The Tiger Who Came to Tea

The Tiger
Who
Came
to Tea

Judith Kerr

CANDLEWICK PRESS

For Tacy and Matty

First Candlewick Press paperback edition 2019

Published under license from HarperCollins Children's Books, United Kingdom

Library of Congress Cataloging-in-Publication Data

Kerr, Judith.
The tiger who came to tea / written and illustrated by Judith Kerr. — US hardcover ed.
p. cm.
Summary: A tiger comes to tea at Sophie's house and eats and drinks everything in sight, so that there is nothing left for Daddy's supper.
ISBN 978-0-7636-4563-2 (hardcover)
[1. Tigers — Fiction. 2. Food — Fiction.] I. Title.
PZ7.K46815Ti 2009
[E] — dc22   2009003658

ISBN 978-1-5362-0962-4 (paperback)

APS 24 23 22 21 20 19
10 9 8 7 6 5 4 3 2 1

Printed in Humen, Dongguan, China

This book was typeset in Goudy.
The illustrations were done in pencil and crayon.

Candlewick Press
99 Dover Street
Somerville, Massachusetts 02144

visit us at www.candlewick.com

Once there was a little girl called Sophie,
and she was having tea with her mummy
in the kitchen.
Suddenly there was a ring at the door.

Sophie's mummy said,
"I wonder who that can be.

It can't be the milkman,
because he came this morning.

And it can't be the boy from the grocer,
because this isn't the day he comes.

And it can't be Daddy,
because he's got his key.

We'd better open the door and see."

Sophie opened
the door, and
there was a big,
furry, stripy tiger.
The tiger said,
"Excuse me, but
I'm very hungry.
Do you think
I could have
tea with you?"
Sophie's mummy
said, "Of course,
come in."

So the tiger came into the kitchen and sat down at the table.

Sophie's mummy said, "Would you like a sandwich?"
But the tiger didn't just take one sandwich.
He took all the sandwiches on the plate
and swallowed them in one big mouthful.
Owp!

And he still looked hungry,
so Sophie passed him the buns.

But again the tiger didn't eat just one bun.
He ate all the buns on the dish.
And then he ate all the biscuits
and all the cake,
until there was nothing
left to eat on the table.

So Sophie's mummy said,
"Would you like a drink?"
And the tiger drank
all the milk in the milk jug
and all the tea in the teapot.

And then he looked round the kitchen

to see what else he could find.

He ate all the supper
that was cooking in the saucepans . . .

and all the food in the fridge . . .

and all the packets and tins in the cupboard . . .

and he drank all the milk
and all the orange juice
and all Daddy's beer
and all the water in the tap.

Then he said,
"Thank you for my
nice tea. I think I'd
better go now."

And he went.

Sophie's mummy said, "I don't know what to do. I've got nothing for Daddy's supper; the tiger has eaten it all."

And Sophie found she couldn't have her bath
because the tiger had drunk all the water in the tap.

Just then Sophie's daddy came home.

So Sophie and her mummy told him what had happened and how the tiger had eaten all the food and drunk all the drink.

And Sophie's daddy said, "I know what we'll do.
I've got a very good idea. We'll put on our coats
and go to a café."

So they went out in the dark, and all the street lamps were lit, and all the cars had their lights on, and they walked down the road to a café.

And they had a lovely supper with
sausages and chips and ice cream.

In the morning,
Sophie and her mummy
went shopping
and they bought
lots more things to eat.

And they also bought
a very big tin of
Tiger Food, in case
the tiger should
come to tea again.

But he never did.